D1408929

BARTLEBY, THE SPORTSCASTER

Ted Pelton

Subito Press | Boulder, Colorado | 2010

subito

Subito Press is a nonprofit literary publisher based in the Creative Writing Program of the Department of English at the University of Colorado at Boulder. We look for innovative fiction and poetry that at once reflects and informs the contemporary human condition, and we promote new literary voices as well as work from previously published writers. Subito Press encourages and supports work that challenges already-accepted literary modes and devices.

Subito Press
Boulder, Colorado
www.subitopress.org

Library of Congress Cataloging in Publication Data
available upon request

978-0-9801098-8-7

Generous funding for this publication has been
provided by the Creative Writing Program in the
Department of English, and an Innovative Seed
Grant from the University of Colorado at Boulder.

Dedication
with thanks, to Neil Schmitz

The author thanks Medaille College of Buffalo, which provided him with a sabbatical leave, during which the final draft of this book was completed.

". . . and yet how feeble is all language to describe the horrors we inflict upon these wretches, whom we mason up in the cells of our prisons, and condemn to perpetual solitude in the very heart of our population."

– Herman Meville, *Typee*, 1841

ONE

With Jake Powell, it was hairpins. He'd been little more than a journeyman and Lord knows what possessed him, but every girl he saw that one summer long ago, Jake would get the hairpin. Never went out and bought a whole bunch of them himself, said that would ruin the luck. And the small black ones, bobby pins, that women might have six or seven or twelve of, those didn't count. No, he was after straight pins, big sharp needles, the kind that looked like weapons. It got so women chatting with the fellas in the hotel bar or outside the ballpark knew what was coming and took off in all directions when they knew Jake was coming. But damned if he didn't get a hit for every hairpin. Two hairpins, two hits, three hairpins, three hits, or so it seemed. He was having the year of his life, the kind of year you can't believe you're having, and most times never comes. At times it got kind of rough for him, trouble with different fellas in different towns. There were some scenes. Ballplayers on the road, you don't need craziness like this going around or else all of a sudden half your team is up on charges from the sheriff of Podunk. People said, "Jake, ease up. You don't need hairpins to hit." But by this time he did. He couldn't do it without hairpins, and was convinced of it. Hairpins, for God's sake.

Jake Powell ended up with 201 hits and at least that many hairpins that year. Not much later he washed out and was never heard from again.

I don't claim to understand it all. Depression is a bear, I know that for certain. From experience, I know, it'll eat you up. You folks out there that don't know what I'm talking about, you've never experienced or encountered it. It's like you don't feel anything, and things that are supposed to feel good, and you know they're supposed to feel good, well, they just don't. You can't help it. There might be something out there that can help you, but you don't know what it is.

Some guys have all the luck. Wade Boggs used to eat chicken before every game, and he ended up with 3000 hits. The old pitcher Ted Lyons used to be called Tex, even though he had no connection with Texas. He just liked it that way, and he ended up in the Hall of Fame. These people are charmed.

Other folks, the far-off look in their eye tells you they don't think they'll ever find what it is that will get them started. Or it might be that they once had it, but now it's lost, and they don't know where they'll ever find it again. They're bewildered. But they don't feel safe having anyone know that. They're unsure. They may be in pain. They may be off someplace in their minds that you can't get to at all. You wonder if they're lying to you. You wonder if it's your fault. It may be – but not entirely. It's happening from within them. They're partially not there.

I've never been depressed myself. Not particularly, like I've seen it happen with some people. Not that I've been particularly charmed either. I've probably had just about as good and bad as anybody.

I know the look because I'd seen it before, in Mary Ann, before I met Bartleby. Mary Ann was my wife, years ago. She was a softball pitcher for the girls team, two years behind me in high school when we first met. She was good – I saw her strike out guys even. The girls' pitcher in softball will suddenly spring out at you, and she was more sudden and surprising with that move than just about anyone, so even though she wasn't lightning fast, she won games. But then she got older—we both got older. I don't know quite how to put it—at some point, night fell over her. Just like that. She kept to herself, sitting alone, staring, whether the lights were on or not, sometimes hardly even getting out of bed, crying a lot. I wouldn't know whether to go to her or leave her alone, and either way was wrong. I guess it had always been there—I don't know. There were so many things.

I was stupid about it a lot of the time, looking back. Anyway, if something might have helped her, it wasn't me, that's for certain. I did fight it in her. I struggled with it. I tried to help her. But it didn't work out.

That was years ago. I do still think about it. I see her smile, the way she was on better days, even in high school. I never remarried.

But a baseball announcer is a happy thing to be. You're always optimistic. Even me, thought I'd seen it all, and then look what happens—the Sox, on the verge of elimination, make the comeback of all comebacks and beat the Yankees four straight!

I hadn't even hoped to hope for it, if you know what I mean. You want something so bad you don't even want to admit you want it, because you know how disappointed you'll be when you don't get it. And then it happens! All of a sudden an everyday outfielder like Johnny Damon becomes Jesus Christ, and has got more people in Massachusetts believing in him than have believed in the Lord in years.

Baseball is big in this part of the country and while I'm not in big-time baseball, I still get paid to remind people of these sorts of things. Always keep people's hopes up. Down by three in the last game, you keep calling balls and strikes like it could break back your way at any moment. It usually won't, as old Billy Buckner will tell you. Ah, poor old Bill Buckner. Still, you say, *Fans, if we can only just turn the corner.* You encourage others to believe. If we can only get our defense in synch with our pitching. We just need those bats to come alive. We've got the makings of a good club here.

Every so often it does happen. Everything clicks into place and a bunch of young kids all of a sudden can do no wrong.

It never lasts, especially since this is minor league baseball. When things go well, it's generally the end. Someone really good gets shipped out to the Toronto or Cleveland before the fans know what number he wore. The New Bedford Arcturions, the double-A team whose games I call, are independent, meaning we're not affiliated with any major league team. It's very much catch as catch can – guys on their way out of baseball for one reason or another, making one last stop, or guys who've latched or here from who knows where, who knows what reason. And not just players. All sorts of weirdos – guys who only shave on one side of their face, schmoozing pseudo-agents gauded up like pimps, big muscle-bound steroid bozos. All sorts of crazies. And corporate horrors in show-fella suits, ice cold right down to the auricles and ventricles. Like Simonelli – but I'll get to him.

Ah, why do I talk so? What's the point? I guess I just can't shut up.

Here then is the story of a very sad case, like I started to say before. One of the saddest, Bartleby. I guess you might say he was just the last new prospect who didn't stick, like a thousand others before him. He certainly wasn't like any of the others. But he was more than just strange. There was something about him, beyond the vacant eyes and general weirdness. Maybe it all happened because of the changes Simonelli brought in. Maybe I'm just a sentimentalist, I like the old ways and I've gotten too old for shenanigans. You can only endure so much pain in the end, or fatigue, or things not going right, and you just want to do something else, be someone else, and then something happens to push you past the limit. That's where Bartleby came in. A catalyst.

Funny, a guy does nothing himself, can do nothing *for* himself, but everything happens because of him. If I could find you again, Bartleby, could you tell me the reason why?

TWO

I can remember my first sight of him at Arcturion Park, our home field.

Morning in a ballpark is peaceful and empty. I more or less live at the place, so I'm up in the pressbox at 8 or 9 in the morning. I've had my own key to the service entrance for years. I get the paper delivered there, *Baseball America, The Sporting News*, even my bills.

Anyway, around eight-thirty in the morning there's José the groundskeeper down on the field and otherwise not a soul in the place. I can see him from where I am, looking at the green expanse of field from above, feeling the early morning coolness of the grass rising up. I can lean out of the pressbox and wave to him, but if I don't, José can't see me. That's the punch line of an old baseball joke, now that I think of it – a guy from Puerto Rico is at Yankee Stadium sitting behind one of the big stadium I-beam pillars. Somebody asks him if he had a good time. "Well, I didn't see the game," he says, "but the fans were so nice. Before the first pitch they all stood up and sang, *"José, can you see . . . "* We've changed that joke around over the years for Dominican guys, Mexicans, Venezuelans, and so on. It's an old one.

Anyway, it's morning and I'm in my own little world here. Our pressbox is smaller than most. The room's only about 10 foot by 10 foot. There's a narrow table against the front wall and a pane of plexiglass looking out on the field. There's two microphones on this table and a computer terminal on my side. Besides that, there's a coffee pot on a small table by the door, a wastepaper basket and a magazine rack. Not much room to maneuver in. By the seventh inning stretch, not only do I have to stretch – I get up and leave the room, walk around the hall for a little while. I get them to play "Take Me Out to the Ballgame" twice to give me enough time to do it. If I don't, my one leg especially, one I broke years ago, starts to act up.

The times between games, mornings like this one, it's been nice since we got wireless in. Perfect for a fella my age, when all you really do is look. It's become another part of my morning routine, you might say. This perfect morning, sunny and not yet too hot, here I am, looking at Amber, probably all of 23 years old. I'm playing and replaying this little movie thing they've got of her, where she starts by walking up toward you and then, well, you get the picture. Not a bad way to pass the morning.

What can I say? Looking at a slender young thing like Amber. Even a fella my age –

Except I hear something. I look up. There's a shuffling coming up the hall, then past the window appears Bartleby. Incurably forlorn Bartleby, struggling toward the door, a computer in his arms, and a pathetic old knapsack over his shoulders, bedroll tied to it in back with string. He reaches the open doorway, turns and faces me. He's pale and thin and there's a line of sweat on his brow, and he's got on a frayed jacket and an expression like the guy who's just been traded to a last place team. He says not a word.

"Land's sakes, fella! You could have gotten José or someone to get a cart and help you with that."

Still not a word, except a quick glance over toward my screen. Not that he can see it from that angle. Still.

"Alright," I said. "Put that down over on your side. This is your spot here." I pointed to the second chair – like we had any room. I tapped the keys to put my computer on screen-saver.

This was the fella Simonelli had fixed up for me.

"What's your name?"

"Bartleby," he answered in a thin voice. No inflection, not even the beginnings of an effort to try to impress me, or to show any life at all. This guy was going on the radio? He had the personality of a turnip!

He finally put down the computer, a shiny, streamlined, one-piece model, certainly spiffier than mine. He found the outlet under the table, plugged it in, booted up. I stood there, silent, watching him. Without another word passing between us, he pulled out the chair and started tapping away on the keyboard.

It made me so angry I had to leave the room. My morning mood was broken. Not only had Amber suddenly become beside the point, but who had taught this guy his manners? Parents don't teach kids any manners these days, and haven't for some time, and this is what results. Now, from April to

September, I'd be sharing what was practically a closet with this kid!

But that wasn't all. I knew Bartleby was being groomed to put me out of work. Mr. Simonelli had let drop that he was going to be bringing someone in. He'd bought the club at the end of the previous year and already you could see all over the place, him replacing this one and that one, getting people who would work cheaper and do things his way. We had new people in the ticket office, a new team bus driver, new security in the parking lot, even new kids in the aisles vending hot dogs, for Pete's sake. Even José, who'd been with the club since the days of Bowie Kuhn, wasn't saying a word, just silently going about his business, afraid to call any attention to himself. Simonelli, according to Simonelli, never made a mistake. Now José and I were the last ones left, besides the players and team personnel.

Bartleby was one of Simonelli's boys.

There was a phone downstairs where I could talk privately. I called Mr. Simonelli.

"Mr. Simonelli, please," I said, when his secretary answered. Simonelli didn't have his office at the park. He owned the company that supplied us with the computers, though they'd seen fit to give me a retread model. He treated the baseball team like it was an annoyance, something that wouldn't be right until he completely changed it. He didn't know the game, didn't even know computers, really. He'd made his name and fortune in cement, then bought Cosmopolitan Computers, a name he'd shortened to Cosmo.

"Yeah," he says when he gets on the phone.

"Mr. Simonelli." I paused a second. No sound of recognition on his end. He knew me well enough. It was a game, always some sort of petty game with Simonelli.

"This is Ray Yarzejski," I said finally.

"Ray," he bellowed. And my head was filled with an image of him, the man I had begun to hate, though I hardly ever saw him face to face. He might have worn suits that cost my monthly salary, but he wasn't much to look at – a stout, fireplug man, with the fat knot of a tie around his neck, self-made and more full of himself than the only rooster on the farm.

He says something like, "So, did you meet Bartleby?"

"Yes I did, Mr. Simonelli." I tried to swallow down my anger and speak calmly, but didn't entirely succeed. "You think a little pipsqueak like that is going to be something the fans like better – "

"Hold on, now, Ray. No need to get all bent. I didn't hire him to compete with you. I got him to do stats and color. I did good by you."

"Color? Don't you have to have a personality to do that? From what I saw –"

"Ray, give it a try. How do you know unless you try? I know that when I'm not right the first time, I try again. When I do that I'm always right the second time, if I wasn't already the first."

Simonelli had a way. You couldn't really believe what he was saying or how he was saying it, and yet you couldn't say so to his face either.

He says, "Hey, maybe he'll turn out to be good luck for the club."

John McGraw used to bring a load of empty "good luck barrels" to the stadium and he was a Hall of Fame manager. He even kept a guy on the roster for three straight years, Charles Victory Faust, who didn't play a game. The guy was around, in uniform, just as a good luck charm.

I used to sit listening to baseball games on the radio when I was a kid. When I wanted extra special luck I'd make myself my favorite sandwich, peanut butter and cold scrambled eggs on toast.

I took my father to a game about a year before he died. It was the first time in many years I had taken a day off and could sit in the stands. He sat watching the goings on with his chin pressed into the box seat railing, looking like an old hound, body sinking, eyes up and watching.

Simonelli was still talking.

"No one's talking about replacing Ray Yarzejski," he said. "Seriously. But you also got to change with the times. I know you like the computers I brought in. You got to admit when I'm right, Ray. Bartleby's a whiz. You're gonna love having him up in the booth. And besides, Ray, you're getting to where you might like the rest. You can't tell me you want to always make every single trip to Pittsfield or Salem. Once he gets his feet wet Bartleby can give you a little time off now and again. I'm always right about people, Ray."

I've always prided myself on being reasonable. I couldn't really say anything until there was something to say.

"OK, Mr. Simonelli," I said. "We'll see how it goes."

He hung up before I did.

THREE

Simonelli had been right about this much. Doing the stats for that night's game, Bartleby was on fire. I called it all myself, but he began feeding me data in inning one and never stopped until the end of the game.

I started out not wanting to give the kid an inch. Every generation always thinks they're smarter than the last. But if that's the case, where did all that we have come from? These stadiums, who built them? How did we get all our little traditions and rituals, the things that give baseball, or anything for that matter, its meaning? Even hot dogs. How did we get hot dogs at the ballpark? Someone a long time ago decided to bring them in the first time. And someone before that ground up meats in a certain way that made the first American hot dog, probably someone adapting a recipe from back in Germany or from my own people in Poland somewhere. Everything we do in life, practically everything we think of to do, we're all just following what has been happening for years and years. That's what the younger folks don't understand. Nothing much really changes, or at least it's best if it don't.

Give me the old timers, every time. Another old Polack like myself, Harry Covaleski, actually used to eat boloney while he was playing and kept a piece in his pocket during games. God bless him. Ty Cobb would file his metal spikes before every game. Rube Waddell would douse his pitching arm with ice water, the exact opposite of what you're supposed to do. It worked for him. Williams, Berra, the Dimaggio brothers – those were some characters.

Still, it's not long before Bartleby starts to win me over. Usually I refer to a daily stats sheet during the game, with some notes beneath about current streaks and what-not. It's generic, put together by the league office. Tonight, Bartleby has added so much material I can hardly digest it all. He's compiled whole new sheets of statistics: home and away averages, breakdowns of individual hitters with runners on different bases, against righties, against lefties, home and away, fielding percentages in various situations, you name it.

I start salivating when I look through it. Sometimes it can get hairy when you've got space to fill during a long at bat with a guy fouling off a dozen pitches. Or during a rain delay, when you've got to keep fans around for forty-five minutes or an hour before we start playing again. This will give us whole new sides to the game to present to our listeners.

It feels Major League.

After the game I tell Bartleby he's done a nice job with the information. I'm still looking down at the printed sheets while I'm saying this. He's also emailed them to me and set up a new team website with all these numbers on it and more. He says nothing in reply.

Did I say something wrong? I look up. Bartleby stares back. I'm brought back to who this guy is – and isn't. He's still paste-faced, washed out, a cipher. When I look at him I feel like I'm looking right through him, like there is nothing there, and I want to readjust my eyes, get some presence to form there. He is small in stature, wearing dingy gray slacks and an exhausted old dress shirt. He doesn't smile or even acknowledge me, just stares. His hair, short and otherwise straight, is kinked out a little on one side and I see heavy circles under his eyes.

A thought occurs to me. "Bartleby, did you sleep here all night?"

He nods.

"Hey, Bart. Take it easy. You don't have to knock yourself out all at once." Despite it all, I realize I like the kid. He's trying hard. He didn't put himself in this spot. He's just grabbing a break that's been offered to him. Wally Pipp sat out one day with a headache and Lou Gehrig played 2,130 consecutive games in his place. Wasn't Gehrig's fault. And he got worse in the end, as it turned out.

So I say something like, "You're OK by me, Bartleby," and I give him a playful bounce on the shoulder.

He almost loses his balance on the chair.

I was saying before about the look of someone depressed, and recognizing it? I saw it there that day. There was nothing in his eyes when I looked at him. You could've shone a light at him and it would keep on going out the other side of the tunnels of his eyes. But what can you do with someone like that? The mind is strange. I think when you see a look like this and you know what it is, experience comes in and tells you what you already know, that you won't be able to do anything for this guy. But your mind keeps you from really registering it and dwelling upon it, if you see what I mean, so that you can keep dealing with them, day to day, and not get in over your head yourself. Put it this way – there's a part of us, when we see someone drowning, that wants to jump in the water and help the person immediately. But then there's also a part of us that breaks away, looks down into the ravine, and holds the rescuer part from jumping into the water to his own death.

Both sides are present in most any normal human being, and say what you will, neither one is better than the other.

That much I understand. What happens next can't be explained.

We beat Salem that night, with me doing all the calls and Bartleby feeding me numbers on each situation that comes up in the games. We do it again Saturday afternoon and then take both ends of a twin-bill Sunday to sweep the four game series. Folks underneath us in the stands are waving a big broom back and forth as we get into the late innings of the last game. It's been a while since I've seen that.

I decide to leave well enough alone and Bartleby off the radio. He shows no particular inclination to talk and when you're riding a winning streak, you don't change a thing.

It's not long before other people notice Bartleby and that our winning started when he got with the team and proclaim Bartleby a good luck charm.

I see José in the parking lot after we finish out Salem. "Choo got to make chure you got everything dee same tomorrow. Keep dis keed doin what he doin."

24

I don't know how you stay twenty years in this country and still hardly be able to speak the language. But that's another story. José's a good egg.

"We're playing good ball, alright," I say. "No doubt about it."

José wags his finger. "Iss not bout ballplay. Dis keed is afortunado." He winks, as if he's just joking. But that's how luck is – you want to keep it, even if it makes no sense, just in case. "We keep afortunado."

The next night it's five in a row. Then six. Like I say, I don't understand it. But I'm beginning to believe it too. This strange kid, with nary a human characteristic besides the ability to tap on a computer keyboard, has lined up everything on the team like a chiropractor straightening out the team spine. Our pitchers are all starting off each opposing hitter with a strike. Everyone's hitting their cut-offs, moving the runner over, and bringing in the guy from scoring position with two outs. No missed signs, no baserunning mistakes.

And just when I like the way things are going and am thinking everything will work out fine, I get a phone call. It's Simonelli.

"Hey, Ray, you old microphone hog. When are you gonna let that boy get a chance on the air?"

"He's good luck, Mr. Simonelli. We can't let him talk yet, not while we're still winning." I start to tell him about my conversation with José, then figure I won't be doing José any favors if I do.

Simonelli loses the smile in his voice. "You're going to put him on for tomorrow night against Pittsfield, Ray. Or else when the team goes to Mystic Friday, what can I say? I got to do what's right for the team."

"What are you saying, Mr. Simonelli?"

"Tomorrow," he says. "Remember, I'm always right. Goodnight, Ray."

Again, I find the receiver still in my hand after he's hung up the phone.

FOUR

It's not good for a sportscaster to fight with management. Players can sometimes get away with it. Especially the good ones, they got something the management can't live without. Sportscasters know, deep down, they're replaceable. I've had a long career myself. But then again, why shouldn't I be able to keep doing what I'm doing? I'm every bit as good an announcer as I ever was. Besides, I've always been a company man. I can change with the times, if that's what's called for. Red Murray once went to the plate for John McGraw with orders to bunt. He hit the game winning home run and McGraw still fined him $100. The team is bigger than just one individual – a bit of wisdom that's especially true when the individual in question isn't too big to begin with.

In the meantime, Bartleby starts going bananas with the statistics – though lifelessly bananas, it's true, because his demeanor doesn't change in the least. But not only does he have spreadsheets with individual breakdowns on how every pitcher has done against very hitter in the league, and vice-versa, but he does something that he endears him to my own heart. He goes back into the history books. Now I know some things about this old team, whose roots go back to when whaling was the primary industry in New Bedford. But minor league baseball is by its very nature ephemeral, here today, gone tomorrow. My own time with the Arcturions goes back to the mid-nineteen-fifties. But as I get older the things I really remember happened when I was a kid, or even before I was born, things I read about. I'm talking major leaguers, Hall of Famers, because when they opened up the Hall of Fame in 1936 I was a youngster and I paid it special attention growing up.

Still, there's not too many people know more about the Arcturions than I do. Arcturus is a star in the Northern spring sky that whalemen used to steer themselves home by after spending winters in the South. Arcturions chart a course home with an eye to the heavens. I've made a lot of hay on the radio with that one over the years.

Bartleby puts me to shame.

Seems there was a pitcher by the name of Ecclesiastes Choate way back in the day who never washed his uniform. Wore a long, gray-streaked beard to go with wild eyes and arms practically down to his knees. Bartleby had the photo of him, pulled from the county historical society archives and scanned, on the team website. Choate had struck out hundreds of batters at the turn of the previous century and never left New Bedford. In the photo, Choate stands posed in the center of a group of fans in street clothes. On the far right is a man with a harpoon.

There was Whalejaw Pete Graves. You couldn't see the inside of his mouth from the photo, but one look at him had you believing the nickname literal. Incredibly, he had played on a false leg, made of ivory. They had made him the special concession, owing to his father having been lost at sea and he himself dismasted as a youngster, or so the story went, of being freely substituted for on the basepaths, provided he reached first. He must have had a mean cut to get any hits at all, though it was said that when he sprang out of the batter's box on his one good leg, got his body out ahead and hopped to catch up with it down the line, he was faster than you'd have thought possible.

To find out all these things, it seemed Bartleby had given up all life outside Arcturion baseball. He was always at the ballpark or doing team business. I was very upset to have to tell him, for Simonelli had made it my job to do so, that he'd have to add the responsibility of the broadcast to everything else. It was another subtle manipulation of Simonelli's. I think he was starting to see that Bartleby – whom he'd never met in person but had simply received reports of from within Cosmo – might not be what he'd thought he was getting. If this proved the case, and he'd made Bartleby my responsibility, he could simply not bring either one of us back next Spring.

So when I saw Bartleby again, shuffling in and plugging his pocket hard-drive into his PC, I told him right out. In fact, I even gave him a little pep talk.

"Okay, kid. Tonight's your night. Mr. Simonelli is looking for big things from you behind the mike, so after I do the opening, we got Pittsfield tonight and we're looking to sweep them out of town and run our streak to seven straight, I'll bring you in, talk you up big. Because you're the one that's turned thing around for us lately, Bartleby, and we'll get Simonelli to see that. I think we can be a good team, you and me. I think you're alright, Bartleby. So, are you ready?"

I had been talking a mile a minute up to this point, trying to get him primed for his appearance, and like I do I even convinced myself, so you could have knocked me over with a pine tar rag when Bartleby looked at me placidly and said, "I'd rather not."

It took me a moment to shake my head of the cobwebs. There was no defiance in his expression. I replayed what he'd said in my mind – rather not – rather not? "Rather not? It doesn't matter what you'd rather do. Those are the orders from upstairs." I examined him closely – still those tired, hollow eyes, that pallor. I had to snap him out of it. "Besides, you're sleeping OK now, right?" He didn't say anything, so I nodded assent myself. "Well, then, this is the job they hired you to do. I'll start off the game and lead you in."

He had no choice, after all. I'd just get into the game and cue to him. It would be dead air otherwise.

I picked up the paper and passed the time until the broadcast. I'd handle it once we got in. But by game time he had me so flustered with his other-worldly lack of expression and emotion that, after 50 years in this business, I made a rookie mistake. No sooner had I started to say, "*Joining me in the booth today as our color man . . . ,*" than I realized I didn't know Bartleby's last name, or if Bartleby was his last name, his first. All I knew him by was Bartleby. "*He's the one who's been pounding out the new numbers you fans have been hearing from me and he's also designed our new team website,*

Arcturions.com. Head over there, fans, and tell 'em Ray sent ya." I was covering for time trying to recall some mention of a second name for him. Nothing, my head was blank. *"The new site has lots of great new features and let me tell you, friends, if you haven't seen it for a while you're in for a very pleasant surprise."* A lot of these new guys, they only go by one name. Like Ichiro, for Seattle. Set a new hit record and all anyone knew him by was the one name, Ichiro. But then we all knew that his full name was Ichiro Suzuki, or Suzuki Ichiro, as it would be if he were still in Japan. *"Yes, and he's going to add a whole new level of excitement to our game calls, that's sure as shootin."* But the rap singers today, they often go by one name usually and put it with some letters, they're all MC This and 2-Shaq That. Could I just give him some letters to make him sound hip? What did I know about hip? *"So let me hand the mike over to my partner in the booth for Arcturion baseball."* I paused, not quite sure what would come out of my mouth next. Gary Carter, the Hall of Fame catcher, always said he didn't have a theory of hitting, except that he hit best when he forgot all the theories. Just do it, the commercial says. *"Here he is – D.J. Bartleby."*

By the time I had gone through all of this I thought for all the world the next words I'd hear would be, *"Thanks, Ray. What a wonderful evening for a ballgame . . . "* But Bartleby didn't say a word.

"Trouble with your mike, eh, Bartleby?" I said, on air, chuckling nervously. *"I mean, D. J.?"*

Nothing.

You can't stall forever in leading up to a ballgame. The Arcturions were in the field and I had yet to set the defense. Our 'r was into his final warm-up tosses. Now we had dead air. So if what I did next seems extreme, keep all this in mind.

I screwed up my throat into the most unnatural position I could, a higher-pitched but still masculine-sounding false voice, far removed from my own deep gravely one, closed my eyes and let out, *"Thanks, Ray. What a wonderful evening for a ballgame."*

Now, I'm far from the most famous man in the history of baseball broadcasting. Only once in my life, as a fill-in, did I ever call a major league game, and that was during a player strike, when replacement players came in and a lot of the regular broadcasters took the opportunity to claim sick leave. But that evening in New Bedford, in a game hardly a soul heard, and two nights later as well, I did something that no other sportscaster in my knowledge ever has. I partnered with myself. *"Redburn got a 3-1 fastball, D.J., and he drilled it into the corner, scoring the Long Doctor, who'd reached on a leadoff walk,"* I'd say in my normal voice. Then, in falsetto, I'd reply, *"As Eddie Stanky used to say, 'Oh, those bases on balls!'"*

"And that's going to be all for Pierre tonight."

"He didn't have his best stuff. 'Lucy, we can't get married yet.'"

"Lucy?" I replied to myself, laughing. Where had that come from? Somehow, in adopting this strange voice and having no time to prepare what I was saying, just going for broke, things were coming out of me that I had no idea were inside me to begin with. *"Who's Lucy?"*

"All the pitchers have girlfriends named Lucy, Ray," my own strange voice answered, deadpan. *"It's a Union rule."*

"And then of course there's Lucy and Desi. Charlie Brown and Lucy."

"Yup, and Wordsworth's Lucy poems."

"What if she should be dead!" I laughed. "Yes, and Lucy in the Sky with Diamonds."

"Isn't the original woman, the origin of all mitochondrial DNA, posited to have been born in Africa some three to four million years ago, called Lucy?"

"If she isn't, she should be. But wherever she is, Lucy is crying now, because Pierre got roughed up tonight, allowing five runs in only two innings and a third, and responsible still for the runner on base, Redburn."

Back and forth like that, with no one the wiser. Truth was, I had always kind of wanted a partner, or thought about having one, and had done dialogues in my mind a million times without realizing it. Now I just let go. Don't get me wrong – I was terrified the entire time! But terror became a kind of edgy excitement, and soon I felt like I was like I was in a place and mood that was comfortable and easy – and brilliant! I was having the time of my life!

Bartleby, the only witness to this strangeness, kept feeding me numbers, his face betraying no emotion.

FIVE

Begging my reader's indulgence for a moment, I am now going to do what a fiction writer is not supposed to do. Forgive me, but I am breaking out of voice, if only for this section. *This is no longer Ray Yarzejski* – the character known by that made-up name. My father had an old friend, and their family was friends with ours, whose name was close to this. I pictured this guy in my mind, but slightly different – and just to begin writing. In time, the character, with this appropriated name, became his own fictional person, different from my father's old friend, based on lots of people I've known, but no one in particular.

Now I am going to see if I can just write real life for a short time.

As I write this, I, the real Ted Pelton, am about to have my divorce from my wife of 13 years finalized.

This has to do with the story, and I'll get to that. Let me tell something of what happened between my soon-to-be ex and I.

If you don't mind, I am going to keep from saying her name. I'll just call her X. There already seems to be lie enough in this so-called act of truth-telling. That is, even in wanting to be forthright and honest, this will be at best a version of events and a condensed one, one that selects a small number of details out of more than a decade – almost two decades – of time. To know the entire story of my marriage and its failure, you'd at the very least have to have X narrate, too. You'd have to have each of us keep from any falsification, even as it might pertain to the lies we told and continue to tell ourselves. Then you'd have to know why each of us did what we did, and that would include other people, other people who very definitely got involved in the story, who would then also each have to narrate, with the same solemn pledge upon them – and this would just provide more perspectives, more of but not the entirety of the story. I don't mean to be obscure or cute or cynical by saying all of this. I say it because I have to, to mark my deep suspicion of any story that ever claims to tell the truth about anything or anyone. All you can hope for, at the very best, is a truth, or some truths, out of many more unsaid – more than one can recognize or tell in one story.

We met in a creative writing program some twenty years ago. I think, at first, I inspired X. I had been writing fiction for a couple of years and had the experience of working with what at the time were called, I think now rather quaintly, "metafictionists" or "postmodernists." There wasn't a narrative in sight I didn't want to explode. I was perennially self-reflexive. I had written a story around that time, for instance, one X used to poke fun at, called "Alfred Says Goodbye." In it, the main character, Alfred, simply says goodbye over and over, to various characters of his acquaintance, in different circumstances, to the most ridiculous extent I could manage, keeping it going and going, and finally somehow getting out of it entertainingly and, of course, self-referentially.

My future wife was a poet when we met. I have never been able to write poetry well; only recently have I been able to write it somewhat passably. I certainly couldn't do it then. Compressed lyric beauty and mystery evaded me, were something I didn't even comprehend. X showed me a poem or two. I didn't understand them. I was very literal. One might say, as a gloss on something more complex and multi-sided, that I lived more in a traditionally male-understood world of accomplishment and goals than did X. I was after something – literary greatness in part, but also simply a job teaching writing somewhere, a certain success that would please my father on the one hand and myself on the other, as I had certainly spurned the directions my father would have had me follow, if he had been making all the rules of my life. I did not have mystical visions. I was not a young Rimbaud. I am surprised, to think of it now again, how businesslike I was about art.

But imagination also moved me. I was in love with the metafictionists, the postmodern makers of narrative. I read all of John Hawkes. I raved about the wonders of Walter Abish, Robert Coover, and my own professors, associates of this group. I read and worshipped Beckett's puzzling, brilliant fictions, and other Europeans and South Americans of the moment: Marquez, Calvino, Borges, Perec, Kundera – and others further back in time: Joyce, Proust, Kafka, Sterne. (All men, you'll note.) I was raving as I met X and others in the workshop. I preached against dogma but was myself very dogmatic and absolute.

Amazingly, X followed my lead. But she wrote in an entirely new way, to my mind. She was not nearly so absolute as I was in my work. Play, *jouissance*, as we knew from our handbook French, our discussions of the theorists so important to our thinking (Barthes, Derrida, Lacan), was something she took to naturally, like a child unencumbered by adult understandings (Rimbaud?), able to simply enjoy the toys at her disposal. She was able to create imaginative worlds, to make magic, to render language slippery and supple, to delve with a world-weary insight beyond her 23 years into understandings of human beings I was still far from appreciating or even observing. I was in awe, and probably frightened.

As another writer of our group at the time said to me a few years later – "You know, X was always the best of all of us." He said it, of course, because he and I were in competition with each other and he would never have given me an inch, nor I him. But he also said it, while I wasn't ready to admit it then, because it was true.

Upon graduation from the Creative Writing Program, she and I, now solidly a couple, looked at PhD programs. Master's degrees in Creative Writing weren't yet regarded as terminal degrees in most places, so unless you were already published (we weren't), getting a good job meant getting a PhD, or at least continuing in graduate school while one tried to write the work that would make me, X, or both of us, famous, deferring student loans in the meantime by staying in school. That was the plan. But now X began to exhibit the signs of malaise and hesitancy that would soon bloom into full-out paralysis in regard to, first, critical writing, and later, any writing at all. In our writing program, X had finished her thesis, the culmination of our two-year degree, with a month-long explosion of writing which resulted in a well-realized novella. No one else had accomplished as much. I thought she would always be able to put things off, wait until the last minute, then explode, succeeding dramatically.

Besides its romance, I was probably overly influenced in this interpretation when my favorite baseball team, the New York Mets, won the pennant and then the World Series in 1986, the year of X's thesis, in just this fashion – stalling, increasing the drama, winning in the end, just when circumstances seemed impossible.

But now the delays began to turn into Incomplete grades in classes. To me, academic work was still all something of a game or a bargain – you did what they had written down for you to do and in the end you got where you wanted to be. But it was a game that didn't interest her, whose reward she was unsure existed and whose stakes she found too onerous to accept. She revised a few earlier works, wrote one or two more stories halfheartedly. She managed to get enough late papers in for grades to get to the dissertation stage.

Let me make clear: these were not tasks of which she was incapable. Quite the contrary. The papers she had written had been singled out for terrific praise, and she had won the respect of one particular theorist on the faculty whose attentions all of our student colleagues were craving. In addition, the department structure having been originally formed during times of campus rebellion decades before, when freedom in all things was the watchword, the actual requirements for the dissertation and the degree were rather soft. It was rumored ıt no one turning in a dissertation had ever failed the defense. Just turn in *something*, we all said to one another.

Nonetheless, it was not uncommon, given these freedoms, for graduate students to succumb to their own demons and invent for themselves difficulties far above what were given to them by the system itself. So it happened with X. She began to write the dissertation, then quit to take a job. Then she quit the job to work on the dissertation. Back and forth she went, able neither to simply give up the task nor conclude it. Are you writing the dissertation? Are you turning back to fiction? *I prefer not to.* In the meantime I had finished my own degree and we'd moved as I got a first temporary job. She was uncertain about her own future, what she wanted. Now, what I had taken to be simply our own lives and difficulties began to reveal themselves to me as being bound up in terrific complexities – familial, chemical, even historical. Her parents, born into the aristocratic and diplomatic circles of old Europe, had lost their wealth and dreams in World War II. X had dealt with abandonment and a routine of despair as a child in this household, born as the youngest child in a sunny California that had no comprehension of the family's hardships, her family's preferred world dead before she came into the world. Her older brother had committed suicide before X was born, and other members of her family spoke frequently of their longings to die. X now began antidepressants and found they only truly worked for her when the standard daily dose was doubled.

At times, I felt the break-up of my marriage had begun before I was born, and that the person truly to blame was Hitler. I understood it all perfectly well. If everything could be taken away, what was the point in doing anything? The previously mentioned "other people" now appeared. Both X and I fucked around. It was the end of the millennium, the President got head in the White House, and I was trying to understand my old ambitions and my new decadence. I reached for something solid – I fell in love with someone else.

As I said, this is but one simplified version of events, and there were more efforts, reversals, pledges, and disappointments to come. More provisions against doubt and despair, more collapsing of those provisions. Like Herman Melville's Bartleby, X began to prefer to remain undisturbed, in the place where she was, with no changes for the present. I began to have new sympathy for the lawyer-narrator in that classic story. I had previously seen him merely as representative of the establishment, with his "snug business among rich men's bonds," failing Bartleby who, revolutionarily, wants desperately to opt out of the limited and false choices offered by commercial, middle-class society. Bartleby was paralyzed by an establishment that offered the Romantic imagination no options – or so I said in my dissertation. But now, as I saw how for years I had tried to offer directions for my sad wife to follow, possibilities for escape from her malaise, I remembered the lawyer. He was imprisoned within conventions, certainly, but he'd also really tried to help Bartleby. He offered to get Bartleby another job, offered to send him to Europe, offered him finally his own home. There is no suggestion in the story that the lawyer is anything but a bachelor who lives alone. The lawyer, in essence, offers Bartleby his own life – shared space in his home, monetary support, companionship of a type others couldn't possibly understand – a type of marriage. Bartleby spurns him. In doing so, Bartleby seems entirely unaware of the lawyer having made any sacrifices on his behalf.

"So true it is," writes Melville, "and so terrible too, that up to a certain point the thought or sight of misery enlists our best affections; but, in certain special cases, beyond that point it does not. They err who would assert that invariably this is owing to the inherent selfishness of the human heart. It rather proceeds from a certain hopelessness of remedying excessive and organic ill."

This isn't all completely analogous. X wasn't unaware that I had made sacrifices for her. In fact, she felt terribly guilty, and this formed the substance of many of our arguments. I also did a great many blameworthy things. I reached a certain point in our marriage's disintegration where I felt released – justified in releasing myself – to do anything I wanted. X never blamed me. I often wish she had. I wanted her to say I'd been a bastard, a cad. Then I could have defended myself. Instead, like centuries of New England ancestors, I found provisional reason to permit myself my desires, acted on them, and never thereafter escaped a certain doubt about my actions.

In any case, X certainly was never as extreme a character as Bartleby. Bartleby does things in the story, like moving into his employer's office, that can only be called crazy. But sometimes the story is so good it becomes the truth. Later, you're not sure if you buy it. Yet, there it is anyway, offering its explanations of events. Then, after a while, the story may become what actually did happen, as far as anyone knows. As what happened disappears, the story becomes all that exists, all that ever existed.

SIX

I wanted to take Bartleby out for a drink after the game but he refused. These kids. Half of them tee-totalers, the other half doing low-carb, though there's not an ounce of fat on them. I was ready to hoist a cold one, perhaps run into a few of the guys from the team. Our streak had now gone seven straight! But no sooner had I left the stadium than my happy spirits faded. Even if I had solved the problem tonight, doing both voices was a high-wire act and there was no way I was going to be able to get away with it for long. I was going to have to do something to bring Bartleby out of it. Strangely, I was feeling guilty about him. Maybe I'd been too competitive with him, given him the cold shoulder, made him feel like he wasn't wanted. We'd gotten off on the wrong foot, but I thought I'd made him feel at home since then – was it possible that he still felt like an interloper, like I was looking at him as the guy who was going to steal my job? Because the truth was, I didn't feel that way toward him anymore. I felt sorry for the guy. I wanted to help him. Why else would I have covered for him like I did? Just to show off? I wasn't showing off for anyone except Bartleby, and he didn't even crack a grin during my performance, even at the most ridiculous moments. But maybe he felt like he'd let me down, and that I was kind of rubbing it in, showing him up, by making out I was him on the radio.

I was all mixed up by the time I got to the house. The phone was ringing. It was Simonelli.

"Hey, the kid was good! D.J.! Who knew? And you said he had no personality. I always had a feeling about him. I always had a feeling."

I now felt an incredible wave of exhaustion come over me, like I'd been steeling up for all of the stressful activities of the whole night and now was cracking open. "Thanks, Mr. Simonelli," I mustered, and tried to end the conversation there. But he kept talking.

"This is going to work out well, Ray. I didn't get that book stuff – I never was much for books – but I'll let that pass. I haven't told you before but we've got TV coverage in the works. Cosmo Computer presents Arcturion Double-A Baseball on WHM-TV. That means TV advertising, promotions, tie-ins with local retailers. Things have never been done right around here, Ray, and we're going to start making a lot more out of this old team than anyone's ever seen. You and D.J. are important here. We'll do the games where you'll start on the TV, D.J. on the radio, and then after three innings, the two of you switch. That way we'll get double coverage, both of you on each station. You'll both do play-by-play. Because I been hearing it already Ray – the fans love this guy. Who ever heard of an announcer who's a good luck charm? You were right – but don't forget who gave you Bartleby in the first place. I'm the one who gets the credit, Ray. Me, Simonelli."

I couldn't believe what I was hearing.

"I'm going to make studio appointments this week for D.J. to start taping commercials."

He would have gone on, but I stopped him. "Mr. Simonelli, why are you telling me this? If you want Bartl – uh, D.J. to do commercials, can't you just ask him?"

There was a brief pause on the line. "Well, Ray, that's just it. I can't get a hold of the guy. I was hoping he was with you. I try the number he's supposed to be at, it must be the wrong one because it says it's disconnected. He doesn't answer his email. I hired him, so I get credit for that, but you're the one who knows him best. I pulled his original employment application with us, and he doesn't even have any family. Under In Case of Emergency Contact, he doesn't have anyone listed. Usually, even if someone's broken with their family, they list someone there, their landlord, a neighbor, someone. It's such a simple thing, but in all of my years in business, with hundreds of employees, I don't think I've ever seen that, not to list a parent or anyone. Our D.J. Bartleby is quite a mystery man."

Simonelli thought this worthy of an abrupt chuckle. I got a sick feeling in my stomach.

I got off the phone.

Spahn and Sain and pray for rain were the by-words of the Milwaukee Braves of the late 1950s. Warren Spahn and Johnny Sain were among the strongest pitchers in the National League in those days.

I pictured that old painting that hangs in the Hall of Fame Museum with the three umpires watching rain fall out of the sky, measuring their decision, a little boy nearby hoping the game isn't called.

I wanted us to have a string of rain-outs. But a rain-out doesn't cancel an appointment to record a radio spot.

I realized I'd been sitting on the couch staring off into space for who knows how long. I felt an old restlessness coming up on me. I don't get this way so much anymore, but every so often the feeling creeps up over me again and there's no putting it off. I wanted some sort of comfort. In the old days, I knew a girl who was sometimes in town I could call, or even certain corners to drive by, doors to knock on. Jesus, I suppose even the younger ones of them were grandmothers now, or worse. Besides, in your own town, there's really never any such thing as anonymity. I've long since given up taking chances like that. I have to say, I do like the internet. But since I'm so much at the park, I never really saw the expense of a separate computer at home. We had a day off the next day before traveling over to Mystic for a weekend series, and now I was wide awake again. It was only a ten minute drive back.

I used my service entrance key and went upstairs to the pressbox. Everything was dark until I got to the plexiglass window in the hall, which let in light from the field-light stanchions. Even the overnight cleaning lady had gone home. I grabbed the knob and started in the door and got the kind of surprise you don't want many of when you're an old man.

The door hit into Bartleby, who was lying on the floor.

He quickly mumbled, "A moment please, I'm occupied," and pushed the door closed. But not before I got a glimpse of what the pressbox had turned into in the few hours since I'd left. They leave about a quarter of the field lights on in the evening, I suppose because it's as easy as turning them on and off and doesn't really cost anything more to leave them burning. Anyway, as I opened the door I could see by this glare the sad man who was my partner in the booth. He was lying on the cement floor on his ratty flannel bedroll, which looked to be some sort of old army surplus, and wearing underclothes, for it was warm enough that he lay atop his bedding, that were equally sad, worn, and torn up, so that he looked for all the world like the very portrait of a dejected, forgotten, terrifically lonely man from some far off hovel at the end of the earth or time. He hadn't a soul in the world and his loneliness gnawed at him like disease, chewing into undershirt, his skivvies, and probably rotting him out from the inside of his chest.

Meanwhile, for the instant our eyes met, Bartleby's face was as blank as ever.

I was so alarmed that I immediately beat a retreat out of the building, as if I was the one whose secret had been found out and exposed. And in truth I felt that way, primed as I had been for a late-night encounter with some porn priestess out in the world somewhere, and finding myself instead confronted by my half-naked colleague in the booth and the knowledge that he was more lonely and forsaken than I would ever be. It was only when I was outside that I realized how sad this man's case was and how much closer to him I felt as a result. For as I've said, I more or less live at the stadium myself. But there was a difference, and an enormous one, expressed by that "more or less." I did have someplace I called home, a small but dignified house, because it's always better to own than to rent, where I raked the leaves, cut the grass, and hung photographs and various bits of memorabilia on the walls. I had a picture of my sister Clare who lives in Cleveland, and her family, my nieces and nephews and grand-nieces and grand-nephew, whom I generally see when the holidays roll around, and who once or twice have come out here to visit me, too. Poor Bartleby apparently had no more to call his own in the world – no, not even a friend – than the bedroll and knapsack I'd seen on his back that first moment he appeared in the doorway carrying the computer that belonged to Cosmo. Maybe he was one of those paranoid cases who kept his money sewed up in his clothing and didn't trust banks, landlords, or television. If that was so, no wonder he was so uncommunicative. Alone and fearful, he had drawn far up into himself. I saw such people all the time – in cities, on street corners, even out on farms, scurrying back behind the doors of houses and barns as I'd driven past. But I'd never actually met one personally.

I went home and decided to treat the moment of sudden shock between us as if it had never happened. I had intruded on Bartleby's private world and every man deserved his privacy, his dignity. Nevermind that his private space was not really private, nor his own. I would also put out of my mind the sight of Bartleby in his most pathetic state. And I would try to make friends with him. Not pressure him, mind you. I didn't want him to become self-conscious and retreat even more. But the truth was, Bartleby was alone and so was I, more or less. We were brothers of a kind. You get used to living on your own and getting along in the world but it's also nice to have someone to share a meal with on the road, or even at home, and to talk about the game. Because like me, Bartleby also was big on baseball. So life hadn't treated him well – there was still who won and who lost, who was hitting and who was mowing

the other side down, and if you cared about those thi
hadn't completely mailed it in yet. There was still, do
somewhere, passion and hope and feeling for one's fellow
human beings.

So I concluded for the moment there probably wasn't as
much difference between Bartleby and I as I had feared. More
truthfully, I think I concluded for the moment to try, as much
as I could, to stop thinking about Bartleby, so I could get some
sleep. I didn't sleep well.

SEVEN

Still, I began the next day determined to try to return everything to normal, as much as possible. I figured I'd hang around the park and then get over to Mystic in the evening, so that I'd wake up there and be ready to prep and call the game in the afternoon. I figured I'd see Bartleby and maybe take him out to lunch, try to shake him out of his doldrums. As one of Simonelli's cost-cutting measures, we were no longer being reimbursed for mileage expenses for away games, it being argued that there was ample room on the new team bus, which featured Simonelli's huge mug across one side on a Cosmo ad twice as large as the team logo on the other side. So I'd also offer Bartleby a ride over, so he wouldn't have to deal with the bus. I love the kids, but even an hour-long road trip with a bunch of twenty-year-olds on a day off was more than I wanted to deal with, and I figured Bartleby with his solitary ways would feel about the same.

I arrived at the pressbox fully expecting to find him there. Where else would he be? So I was almost as surprised to not discover him there as I'd been to find him on the floor the night before. To the side of the large pane of plexiglass was a small pivoting window, like the kind you used to see in the backseats of cars. This was open, no doubt to give the place some air. Underneath the long front table, on Bartleby's side, I saw his bedroll and knapsack. I couldn't resist. I waited a few moments, then, hearing nothing, took out the knapsack and opened the top. Inside was everything I supposed the fella had in the world. It wasn't much more than clothes – some dirty, some clean, but all loose and threadbare. Near the top was a large ball of paper, which, as I pulled it apart, turned out to be nothing more than a wad of thin hot dog sheets – about a dozen altogether. It seemed that this was just about all about he ate. Otherwise, his possessions were more notable for what they didn't contain. There were no photos of any kind, no address book or machine equivalent, no personal effects except a toothbrush and a comb, no letters and papers, save one folded up piece of paper, addressed to him care of Cosmo Computers, a three-line notice that he had been hired to do statistical work and broadcasting for the New Bedford Arcturions, and that while the club knew he hadn't had any previous broadcasting experience, the letter went on, they were certain he'd make the most of his opportunity, having shown what a committed employee he'd been in his time with Cosmo. The wording had the sound of something that had been cooked up first somewhere else and then warmed up in a microwave, so that there were still a couple of cold spots here and there. It was signed at the bottom, Enzo Simonelli.

Well, says a lot about my contributions to the team, I thought to myself. They'd hired a guy to replace me who'd seemingly never even done an audition tape. I stood for a moment, the letter still in my hand, the knapsack on the table, the bedroll on the chair seat. I turned around. It was Bartleby.

"Hey, Bartleby," I said. He looked at the table and my hands. I folded the letter back up and put it with his things.

"I'm sorry, kid. I didn't know what it was. You can't be too careful about unattended packages these days, like they're always telling us. I just wanted to make sure no one was doing something to mess with this winning streak we're on, huh, kid?" I tapped his shoulder, as I had once before. He didn't stumble this time. Stone-faced as ever, he remained looking at the knapsack.

"Ah, kid," I said. "I just want to do right by you. What do you say we go grab a bite to eat before heading over to Mystic? My treat."

He blinked slowly and looked at me. "I'd rather not," he said.

He was probably particular about his diet, like they are nowadays. In the old days, guys would scarf down whatever you put in front of them, and chase it with three or four beers. With how pale this kid was, he could use it.

I'd seen the hot dog wrappers. "You want to go downstairs and get a couple dogs then? They have them hot in the big kitchen a lot of times even when we're not playing."

"I'd rather not."

"Sure, OK, I understand. You want me to come back here and pick you up for Mystic?"

"No, I'd rather not go to Mystic."

He really was going to make me pay. "OK, your choice. But they're a rowdy bunch on the bus. But OK." He was still mad at me and I couldn't really blame him.

"I'd rather not go on the team bus."

Then he had his own car.

"Well, I'll see you over there, then. Say, around 4:30? You know how to get there."

"I'm not going to Mystic."

"Oh, come on, Bartleby. Don't be like that. I'm sorry I did this." His things were still on the table in front of me and I began to put them back together. "But you know, Simonelli's right. This is a good opportunity. He's got things planned."

"I'd rather not be part of his plan."

I studied Bartleby closely. Was he doing this for me? Maybe he didn't want to be part of putting me out to pasture. It was only last night I'd covered for him during the game, when he'd lost his nerve, and while it seemed like two weeks ago after what had transpired since, it had obviously had an effect on him. He wanted to go to bat for me.

"It's not like that, Bartleby. Simonelli's told me he's got room for both of us." But I wasn't sure if I believed that myself. Maybe Simonelli was just playing me, telling me something he thought I might want to hear, so that I would encourage Bartleby until he could replace me. It didn't matter. I liked the kid. It was probably getting near time for me to hang 'em up anyway. I could come back on special occasions, or just do home games, like Harry Caray used to at the end of his time with the Cubs. Maybe they'd even have a Ray Yarzejski Day.

Bartleby eyed me dully. He was so sad that I wanted to reach down deep in myself and find something to give him, some sort of comfort to make up for my betraying him, invading his belongings. "Look, Bartleby, don't worry about Simonelli. Because guys like that, they're never going to be bigger than what it is we do here." I pointed out through the window, out of the field. There was a blue tarp on the infield, but otherwise it was green and inviting. Looking at a baseball diamond always fills me with hope and joy. "Look at that out there, Bartleby."

He looked past me slightly, so that I could see the field was in his vision.

"That's what this is all about, Bartleby. We call baseball games. You were the one who told me about Ecclesiastes Choate! That guy would have been nobody all his life, a complete misfit, and forgotten about the moment he died, except that he played baseball. Now he lives on. You're a part of that, Bartleby." I had been looking at Bartleby but now I turned around and looked again at the field, pristine and emerald. They'd let the grass grow while the club was out of town, let the turf recover a little bit before firing up the mowers and lining it fresh again for when we got back into town in a week. But I couldn't see a thing wrong with it, and I've always had good eyes, only needing a prescription for reading. A baseball diamond is always perfect.

"Come on, Bartleby," I said. "We got a game to call in Mystic."

"I'd rather not," said Bartleby. "I've given up baseball."

In 1957, when Hammerin' Hank Aaron was just coming beginning to be a star with the Braves, they got to the World Series against the Yankees. Yankees catcher Yogi Berra figured he'd have some fun with the kid. Berra pointed out that Aaron had the trademark on the bat turned the wrong way, toward the pitcher, which is said to be a way you crack your bat.

"You're supposed to look at the trademark, kid," said Berra.

"I ain't up here to read," snarled Aaron.

You can't make a fella hit. They're either up there to do it or they're not. I could do nothing with Bartleby. I shrugged and left. To tell you the truth, and though it makes me feel terrible to say this, I was to the point where I was glad to get out of there. Giving up baseball! I was shaken. I walked right out to my car, without pause, as if my stopping would entangle me in further problems. I was worried I'd run into José, and he would somehow know everything and the next words out of his mouth would be, "So what are jou goin to do bout Bartleby, Señor Afortunado?" Or I expected Simonelli to bruise his way past a stadium attendant and grab me, "Did you tell Bartleby what we've got planned for him? My plan can't fail, tell him." I didn't want any of it. I got to my car, got inside, and got out of there and didn't even stop for a bite but hit the road for Mystic directly.

I called the game that night again the same way, doing the absent Bartleby's lines for him and hoping to talk myself into a better frame of mind. It was dreary. Rain stopped the game twice and I had to fill in space. My heart wasn't in it. I sent Bartleby's voice off in the fourth inning, claiming he was under the weather. Everything seemed to go wrong in the game as well, the entire team suddenly inept again, errors aplenty and the Mystic bats hitting everything in sight. I felt like it was all my own fault. I wished I hadn't spied on Bartleby and, having tried to make good, hadn't beaten such a hasty path out of there. Bartleby was lost, and I needed to keep him with me to keep him OK.

No sooner had the last out been made – a 12-2 thrashing, ending our winning streak at 7 – than the phone rang in the Mystic booth. Stupid me, I've never learned not to pick up the damn thing. It was Simonelli.

"Ray, what the hell is going on?" he shouted.

"Mr. Simonelli," I said. I loudly fumbled through some papers, trying to buy time. I decided to play innocent. "Well, I guess you can't win 'em all."

"Ray, I don't know who you got calling the game with you, but I know it's not Bartleby. Bartleby's at Arcturion Park. José tells me he's taken up residence in the booth."

"Yeah, well, Bartleby's kind of a sad case." I felt like I was selling him down the river, and I couldn't do that. "But I can work with him. I'll bring him along and he'll be fine. I'll come back to New Bedford tonight and get him."

"No need. I had the police take him away. He was a damn lunatic. He was sleeping at the Park. I'm not hosting a lonely hearts club here. I've got a company to run."

Tommy LaSorda used to say, when he managed the Dodgers, "I like coming to work every day, you never know what's going to happen." He never had a job outside baseball. Neither had I hardly, except for my off-season work and some Amway and the like to make ends meet.

"You know, Enzo." No one called him by his first name and I'd been told he didn't like it. "You're going to rot in hell."

"That's an awfully big stone to throw there, Ray, unless I'm mistaken, which I'm likely not. An awfully big stone. Especially for a guy like you who likes to use the internet."

It figured that Simonelli would know where I went on the internet, though it hadn't occurred to me before.

"You want I should finish out the series here in Mystic."

"I think you're going to have to go immediately, Ray. I've got a thousand guys who'll take your spot in a heartbeat, and I've also got to think about how I'd withstand community pressure. I'm changing things for the better around here. How do I justify keeping a pervert like you?"

For a third time, I found myself holding the receiver after Simonelli had already gotten off the phone.

And thus, unceremoniously, after fifty years, ended my career in baseball.

There will never be a Ray Yarzejski Day.

EIGHT

For years, I'd never known anything but the ballyard. Now I was suddenly a widower. I had a little money socked away. I thought of immediately going to a travel office and getting a ticket somewhere. But where? Who wants to fly to the Bahamas and end up alone there, bawling? What would be the point of that? Nor am I a drinking man, so I wasn't about to crawl into a bottle for a few days of forgetfulness. There would be no forgetting.

Besides, I've come to the conclusion over the years that the easiest way of life was the best. That's why I more or less swore off women years ago, after being married the one time. It all seemed to me more trouble than it was worth. I even stopped trying to chat up women in bars. There was no point. Even if you got lucky, after the fireworks and the smoke cleared you always ended up with a person there with you – that person's needs and sadness and problems. No, in the years since Mary Ann and I went our separate ways, I've generally been happy to live my life among men. It's been a lot easier that way. The different parts of my life stay in their different compartments. About those years before, there's not much to say. I wasn't very successful at being a husband. At the same time, it would have been hard for anyone to live with someone they could never make happy – someone constitutionally unable to get out of an overwhelming funk. What can I say? When all you get back is disappointment upon disappointment, after a while you start to look elsewhere.

Now, none of this had been on my mind for quite some time, but that evening, having gotten back from Mystic, all of it started coming back to me. It hurt to get canned by Simonelli, sure. Still, I'm not one to mope about things that have happened or to spend too long thinking about what might have been. I'd seen it coming, and I'd had a long run. It's always on to the next thing, with me.

But when you've been doing one thing for a long time, it's not like you can flip a switch and suddenly enter a new life. I tried sleeping but I couldn't. I got up and put on the TV, but I wasn't really watching it and before long all of those voices and noise made me just turn it off. I tried going back to bed and after awhile I heard my old chiming clock go one and curiosity kept me wondering what time it was until I heard it go three, meaning it was now 3 am and had been 2:30 the first time, because the clock chimed once on half-hours. Though I'd at least been a little drowsy before, now I was completely awake.

My bedroom is in the upstairs part of my house and now, up and about, I went like in a trance to where the rope hangs from the ceiling in the hall and I pulled down the staircase to the attic, without even thinking about the ridiculousness of such a thing at such an hour. The stairs dropped down, flimsy metal runners and wood slats that pitched to one side as I climbed up. They were a horror to get up – it had been at least a year since I had gone up there and I didn't remember them as being so rickety, and I've also put on some weight. But I made it. Once in the attic, where I could stand straight only in the center, I picked up the flashlight that I keep up there. Luckily, it still worked. I found my way to a near corner and what I had come after, the old shoeboxes full of pictures. I took up the largest boxful, that I knew held the oldest photos. Managing to get down the stairs out of the attic without killing myself, I took the box all the way downstairs to the kitchen table, where there was good light, and started flipping through them.

There was a picture I knew I'd find there, an old picture Mary Ann had given me more than sixty years before, when I'd gone in the service. It was an old 1 1/2 by 3 inch black and white. In one corner she had written, "I love you. I am yours," in slender curling letters in the washed out ink of an old fountain pen. I turned it over. Her writing covered the back.

> This was taken
> the day I graduated
> from 10th grade.
> Don't loose it. It
> is the only one I
> have. It isn't
> very good but I
> had on your
> favorite dress.
>   Oct. 4, 1943
> I love you.

She stood against a hedgerow and the bright sun made black shadows on her face around her eyes and mouth almost like a cut-out mask. But even with this, it was her youth that overwhelmed me – her apple-cheek roundness and freshness. This was before we had become lovers in the physical sense, which wasn't until I came home from the war. The gray blurs of houses in the background could have been any houses, but I recognized them as the ones from the street behind my parents' house, the house I grew up in, the old neighborhood in Connecticut.

I picked up another picture. It was bigger, on thicker paper, and faded brown. Mary Ann was posed on the wooden front porch of her house, or rather, her folks' house. She was a year older, 18, I believe. Mary Ann was always a big girl, an athlete back in the day. Here, she looked like the goddess of the hunt – is it Athena? Diana? Slender young muscles bulged in her legs. She posed like this for me, lounging – sexy, but also innocent. We were such innocents in those days! She sat back in her skirt with her legs crossed at the ankles, elbows resting on the threshold of the open door. Her lips were cherry red with lipstick (the photo wasn't in color, but I *knew*), and half-pursed in a smile, like she would be blowing a kiss at me a second after the shutter clicked. Her wavy hair was pinned up on one side and her skirt was pulled up just above her knee. She wore a tight sweater and the way she held her arms back and thrust out her chest stretched the material and whitened the tops of her breasts.

Dozens of photos were in this box, from years of my life, loose and scrambled together. I looked for a long time at one, trying to figure out where it had been taken. It was a pick-up ballgame and it was in color, but blurry. It was taken at some neighborhood field, close up enough that you coulc tell something big was happening in the game, as seen from the third-base dugout area. A runner was making his way from second to third as the fielders all faced in the other direction, looking toward the unseen ball in a vague, yellow-green outfield. The right side of the picture was black from exposure. I had no idea who the teams were, nor any of the players. It was some summer, some game not in any league, a bunch of guys having fun. It was a game I'd probably played in, and someone had likely given me the picture. I was damned if I knew who.

And then it came to me. It was a softball team I played with one year, but hardly played at all because I had broken my leg sliding into a base. I had taken pictures that day, half in the bag, sitting with my leg in a cast propped up on the beer cooler.

I also paused long over a picture of a cat from just a few years ago, a white female named Patti. She was laid out stretching on the couch in a beam of sunlight. Cats always know how to pose, somehow. This picture was only about ten years old. I had taken it intending to give to my eldest niece's little girl when I saw them, but since I still had it, I guessed I must not have given it to them. I'd brought Patti home from the park – I don't know where she came from, but she lived by one of the dugouts and sometimes would run out during play – particularly if she saw a bird. She couldn't stay there and no one else volunteered, so I decided to take her home and try out having a cat for a while. She was a very sweet companion, and continued to a good birder in my backyard, staying with me about ten years. But when she died, I decided not to get another one. I felt bad I had to leave her alone so often, and I didn't want to feel responsible.

ow what came over me, because I probably hadn't

hen she actually passed on, but I began to cry

atti stretched out so serenely on my old couch.

. ....as just death itself, I don't know. But something about seeing her there alive and thinking how it had been years now that she hadn't existed in this world, and how the world goes on without us, and I hadn't even given her a thought for years and I was the only one she saw for years, the only one who would give her a thought, and probably because I was just so tired, I first started to tear up and then began weeping, uncontrollably, gushers coming out of my eyes.

The first rays of light came up and I'd had enough. I said to myself, out loud, "Stop being a damned fool." I got myself a glass of water from the kitchen tap and wenvvt back upstairs to the bedroom and lay on the bed for about an hour. Then I got up as I normally would on a night-game-day, at 7:30. I showered, shaved, and dressed. I stopped in down the street at Betty's for coffee and breakfast, just like any other day. I got the paper, said hello to all the folks, and pretended for everyone's benefit I'd had a peaceful night's sleep and that it was a great day to be alive in the world.

NINE

From breakfast, I went straight to the downtown police station, where there are also holding pens. I needed to help Bartleby out – who else would? But Bartleby was no longer there. They'd had him, they said, but if it was the fellow they thought I meant, he had gotten into a scuffle with one of the officers as soon as they brought him in and been sent to Springfield.

"Are you sure we're talking about the right guy?" I asked the officer on duty. "Bartleby." I spelled it. "He'd never hurt a fly."

He looked me over. Though I was making out everything was normal, I probably looked terrible. I had cut my chin shaving and hoped it wasn't bleeding.

"I'm Ray Yarzejski," I said. And then, hoping it might help, "The Voice of the Arcturions."

"Sure," he said, non-committally. He flipped a couple of pages in a big log book, probably thinking I was some sort of nut-job. He wore the blue uniform of the local police. I dabbed at my chin with my handkerchief. The blood had dried.

"Bartleby – what's the full name?"

"I don't know."

"Is Bartleby his last name or his first?"

We went around like this for a while. I even volunteered the possibility he might have been booked as D.J. "Springfield," the guy told me again finally, though I wasn't sure he actually ever located Bartleby's name.

I got up to Springfield that afternoon, not wanting to lose any time, but they had never heard of Bartleby. The guard at the desk there told me it wasn't surprising. The jail there was beyond capacity and a lot of the new inmates, especially for violent offenses, were being shipped to any number of facilities, a lot of them out of state. In Kentucky and Texas, for instance.

"He's not in for a violent offense," I said.

The guard waved this objection aside. I hated him immediately. He was as fat and full of himself as Babe Ruth at Christmastime. "What you want to do is go back to the original jurisdiction and see if you can find out where they sent him."

"You're sure he isn't here."

"He could be anywhere by now. By definition." I wasn't sure what he meant by that, but he seemed proud of his phrase. His gray uniform shirt showed big sweat circles under the arms. "One place your Bartleby is not," he told me, "Is here."

When I left, he was using a letter-opener to stab another donut from the half-eaten box on the desk.

It was all ridiculous, but would get even worse. When I got back to New Bedford, it was past 4:30, and they wouldn't tell me anything. The person who knew – evidently the only person trusted to know anything there – had gone home for the day. So it was the next day before I could tell anyone Bartleby wasn't in Springfield. Again, they took out the big log book. The guy flipped back a couple pages, then went to get another book. Finally, he turned up something – a guy who was signed in as Elbee, Bert.

"I wasn't here to take this one in. He's been transferred to extended detainment."

"Extended detainment?"

"Due to the overcrowding, we've had to farm some out. Good people who are doing this for us, though." He gave me a half-smile of envy – I was getting to see the newest thing in jails before he had.

He pulled out a packet from under the counter. There was a card and forms to fill out and send to a company called IncarcerNation.

I put them in the mail and in another week heard back from IncarcerNation. There was a record of a Bert Elbee going to the Dallas County Regional Correctional Facility, and there was a phone number. A computer voice had me key in 1 for English and the number corresponding to the last name of the inmate about whom I was inquiring. I put in 3, E, for Elbee. There was no Elbee. I keyed and heard a listing for a Donald Elber, from Virginia. I got back to the letter listing and tried 2, B, for Bartleby. There was no record of a Bartleby from any state. I went back to the menu and after waiting through some piped in music, finally got someone live, a woman with a chirpy midwestern accent.

"Could you look up other variations on the spellings?" I asked after she tried both Elbee and Bartleby without luck.

"I can only process names where forms have been filed, sir."

"I listed different possible spellings very clearly in the margin of the form I sent in."

"A new spelling of a name requires a new form, sir."

"But how can I know how his name might have been misspelled?" I thought of the staff at the two jailsites I'd seen. Did you have to finish high school to be a cop or to work in a jail? High schools nowadays, did it matter? I wouldn't trust any of these people to write down their *own* names correctly.

"You can also fill out this form online," she told me, something of a non-sequitur.

"I don't have access to a computer."

"Each claim will be processed as it is received," she chirped, then continued after a pause, "IncarcerNation is committed to the highest levels of quality assurance. Have I answered all of your questions?"

I lost it. "Quality assurance! You've told me nothing! I don't have any idea of where to look. My friend was picked up, I assume on a vagrancy charge, in New Bedford, Massachusetts, and first I'm told he's in Springfield, then I'm told he's in Dallas, Texas, and maybe he's in Virginia. Nobody's taking responsibility!"

"Please don't yell at me, sir. We service a great many customers and you don't even know this man's name. If you go to our website, you can download the form you need to fill out as a PDF and you can fax it to me personally. You can fax me as many forms with as many different spellings as you want. Should I give you the fax number?"

"I don't have a fax."

"I can send you the forms in the mail." She repeated my address back to me. I heard a couple of computer clicking sounds on the line. "IncarcerNation is committed to the highest levels of quality assurance. Have I answered all of your questions?"

"Yes," I said, not knowing what else to say.

"Thank you, sir. You have a nice day."

I hung up the phone and looked out the window. I felt like I was waiting for a phantom to appear.

Just who was Bartleby, anyway? Where had he come from? I didn't know. He had simply turned up somehow in the Cosmo organization. It was no use asking there; the way Simonelli did things, now that Bartleby was an ex-employee, he would have no history there – probably no one would have been at Cosmo long enough to tell me anything. From what I knew, he had made headway at some point in the corporation, doing work that called attention to himself. But I don't think Bartleby ever wanted that. I think he merely got good at computers and did was he was told. The last thing I think he ever wanted was to be noticed. Something had to have happened to him long ago to make him want to bury himself in a faceless organization, to become another piece of nondescript data in a sea of lost numbers. Cosmo, its partitioned desks and cubicles, probably seemed a comfortable enough place to him, a place where everyone would leave him alone while depression (or whatever you want to call it) slept inside him, occasionally waking and gnawing away more of his insides.

But no one deserved to be lost to the world. No one had the right to swallow someone up like that. Who was there to defend Bartleby? Who would stand up for him – or even try to find him? Simonelli himself had told me he knew nothing about Bartleby, Simonelli who found out everything about everyone. Simonelli seemed to have never even met Bartleby. Who besides me was there to say Bartleby even existed?

What else can I do at this point? I'm closing up the house for a while. I'm driving to Texas. If I need to, I'll head back to Virginia from there. Or wherever.

I'm just not really good for sitting around anymore. I'm getting checks for the rest of my contract for the year. I half-suspected Simonelli would try to weasel out of it, but he simply washed his hands and I got my money. This and social security gets put in the bank. It's enough to give me all I need, gas, a cheap place to stay. Sometimes I just sleep in the car.

Do I think I'll really find Bartleby? I don't know. Someone should look for him, is my feeling. But I tire easily. I don't really go very far each day. I seem to get lost. I don't know why. I've got a good car, a late-model Buick Century with cruise control, and I've gone back and forth for years from New Bedford to Salem to Mystic to wherever, making good time, no trouble at all. But now I look up and I'm heading back East or North, where I just came from, and I've gone eighty or a hundred miles or so in the wrong direction. I stop and get coffee and turn around. It doesn't seem to help much. I do it again.

I guess I'm not in an awful darn hurry.

Partly, I wonder what's the point. Why do I want to find Bartleby? I've never done him any good, nor he me, when you think about it. I don't know what I'll say to him if I do find him. I'll probably tell him I was sorry, though I'm not sure for what. Or maybe I'll get to Texas and it'll be some other guy, named Elbee or Elber. I'll sit down and talk to him if he's willing, having come all that way. I've never talked to a murderer. It might be interesting. At my age, what have I got to lose?

I drive. Sometimes I get listening to some radio program, some damn thing, and I get madder and madder. Some of these things just lie and lie. People just eat it up. I'm sorry for all the years I spent deceiving people. These little towns, pointless eruptions of houses out of the space and emptiness. Love's gone bad, business gone bad, town's gone bad. Voices, as if they come right of the houses, come right into my head. "I borrowed money from my father-in-law, who's a well-known judge, and I don't know how I'll ever pay it back." "Ma, you wouldn't believe it, they're bringing in Christians by the busload to see Jesus get his ass kicked." "Admit it – you're just going to do what you want in the end, like you always do." "Leave me alone, I just want to die." Finally, just when everybody's gotten used to the misery, a robber-baron rides into town and changes what most everyone always took for granted, in ways they never thought of, so now they're even worse. Listen to the radio and you keep hearing how things are great or have gotten better. You can buy this thing or that thing. They just keep smiling and telling us to wait for the big rally. I used to be one of these people. There's always tomorrow. If we could just wake up those bats. If we could just turn the corner.

We're never going to turn the corner. There is no corner.

I had a dream about Bartleby a few nights ago. I had found him in a cell in somewhere like Nebraska, someplace I've never been. He looked the same as he always had, which though it wasn't good was it least a comfort. Only one thing was actually new about him. With him in the cell was a strange dark bird that was no particular species I could describe. It had broad chest of an eagle, but was darker, like a hawk, and low-necked, like a vulture. It was also hulkingly large, nearly as large as Bartleby himself, which makes me think now that it couldn't have been on his shoulder but must instead have been on a perch in the corner of the room. It might have been in both places at the same time, the way things sometimes are in dreams. I sat on a chair across from Bartleby and leaned toward him, concerned. I really did want better for him.

"Bartleby," I said. "It's good to see you." I wanted to make the best of the situation. "Hey, this isn't so bad." I nodded to the bird. "They let you keep pets in here, at least."

He met my eye, slowly, emotionless, the way Bartleby did. "I know where I am," he said, and turned back away.

It's true: a person can sit in the sun all day and get watered well but not know quite how to grow right, like a bad plant. But then I wonder what makes a Simonelli, who sees other people in the world as so much fodder for his own greed? What makes ambition such that it only sees itself, and persistently hurts anyone else who comes in contact with it?

In a deep darkness, out in the country, I start up again. No highway lights or rest stops or houses or farms. Three or four in the morning, before anyone is awake for the new day. The centers of towns are vacated. In the countryside, there aren't even farm animals out. That's from fear of carnivores, is what that is. From the time I was a young boy, I always knew I'd get eaten alive. I used to have nightmares about it. A fella I know met up one time with a bear while hiking. The bear looked at him and, after a second, headed the other way. The story only frightened me all the more. Because you never know. It's likely there's something out there, something bigger than us. It doesn't have to be hungry to be always eating. It doesn't help that you've escaped it before – you may not be lucky this time. You lose everything, no one pulls the plug for you at that point – you keep on moving, waking, thinking, though no one tells you in what direction. You are never allowed, even after losing it all, just to sit in one place and not do anything. People wouldn't put up with that. They'd keep pushing and prodding and eventually get angry, until you start moving again.

Then there's folks like me who wouldn't be happy sitting still. Just got to keep moving. I'm sure things will all work out fine. They'll be fine, fine.

Ah, Bartleby. Ah, humanity!